Joshua ben Perahiah would say:
Find for yourself a teacher, choose for yourself a friend,
and judge everyone with the scale weighted in their favor.
– Pirkei Avot, 1:6

But Perhaps, Just Maybe...

To my beloved mother and father: Thank you for the abundance
of opportunities and the constant embrace of love.
TDO

To my beloved family, from whom I learned to look
at the world with loving eyes.
MH

Green
Bean
Books

First published in Israel in 2020 by Yedioth Books
First published in the UK in 2021 by Green Bean Books
c/o Pen & Sword Books Ltd
47 Church Street, Barnsley, South Yorkshire, S70 2AS
www.greenbeanbooks.com

Green Bean Books edition: 978-1-78438-736-5
Harold Grinspoon Foundation: 978-1-78438-740-2

Designed by Ian Hughes
Edited by Julie Carpenter, Sophie Judge & Susannah Okret
Production by Hugh Allan

Printed in China by Leo Paper Products Ltd.
0122/ B1838/A6

MIX
Paper from
responsible sources
FSC® C020056
FSC
www.fsc.org

But Perhaps, Just Maybe...

Written by Tuvia Dikman Oro

Illustrated by Menahem Halberstadt

Translated by Gilah Kahn-Hoffmann

Green
Bean
Books

It was a beautiful morning.

Duck and Hedgehog wheeled their
bicycles out of the shed and discovered
that Duck had a flat tire in the front and
Hedgehog had a puncture in the back.

The two friends set out for Mrs. Hoopoe's
Bicycle Shop.

They walked along the path, enjoying the warm, sunny day.

Suddenly, they heard a loud rattling noise behind them. Cat zoomed past on her red motorcycle, driving around them and raising a billowing cloud of dust.

Duck coughed and looked annoyed: "My eyes are stinging from the dust. Horrible cat! She should have some consideration for others!"

"But perhaps, just maybe," suggested Hedgehog, "she's rushing off to help her sister, who fell and sprained one of her whiskers."

Duck preened his feathers and said, "Maybe, and maybe not."

The friends shook off the dust and continued on their way to Mrs. Hoopoe's Bicycle Shop.

And then, right there in front of them, was Mr. Billy Goat, rolling a gigantic rock into the middle of the path, waving hello and then hurrying away.

"Now this?" grumbled Duck. "What is Billy Goat doing? He's blocked the path. We can't get by! That Billy Goat really irritates me!"

"But perhaps, just maybe," suggested Hedgehog, "Mr. Billy Goat saw a big hole in the road and sealed it off so no one would fall in."

Duck scratched his feathers and complained, "Really, Hedgehog! What a silly idea. He's just being annoying!"

The two walked on toward Mrs. Hoopoe's Bicycle Shop.
It was a long way, and the friends were tired and hungry.

"I know. Let's stop and eat some raspberries from the bush
that grows at the top of the hill," Hedgehog suggested.

"Great!" Duck replied. "I'm crazy about raspberries."

The two friends walked across the hill until they came to the raspberry bush. But who else was there? Mrs. Fox.

She was holding a basket filled to the brim with raspberries. She plucked the last raspberry from the bush, waved goodbye, and hurried off.

"Darn! Darn! And double darn!" shouted Duck. "Did you see that, Hedgehog? Mrs. Fox picked every last raspberry. I am so angry!"

"But…" Hedgehog began.

"Don't even start!" groused Duck.

"Perhaps…" whispered Hedgehog.

"Perhaps what?" asked Duck.

"Perhaps, just maybe, she saw that all the raspberries were very ripe, and she picked them before they could spoil, to share them with friends."

"Really?" griped Duck, and he kicked at a small stone. "It doesn't work that way, Hedgehog. Don't you, 'but perhaps, just maybe' me!"

The two walked on in silence until they reached Mrs. Hoopoe's Bicycle Shop.

Sitting at the entrance to the shop were the two cat sisters.

"Hello, Duck. Hello, Hedgehog. How nice to see you. I apologize for not stopping before to say hello. I was in a hurry to reach my sister. She tripped and sprained the tip of her whisker. But now she's fine. So if you were worried, thank you."

Duck turned to his friend Hedgehog in astonishment, but before he could say a word Billy Goat emerged from the shop, chewing on some oats.

"Hi, Duck! Hi, Hedgehog! It's nice to see you. I was just telling Mrs. Hoopoe and Mrs. Fox about the pit that opened up in the middle of the path and the huge, heavy rock I found to fill it in. No one will fall into it now. Would you like to wait here with me until Mrs. Hoopoe finishes putting a new chain on my bicycle?"

"Sure," said Hedgehog as he held out a hand to steady Duck, "but let's just tell her that we're here."

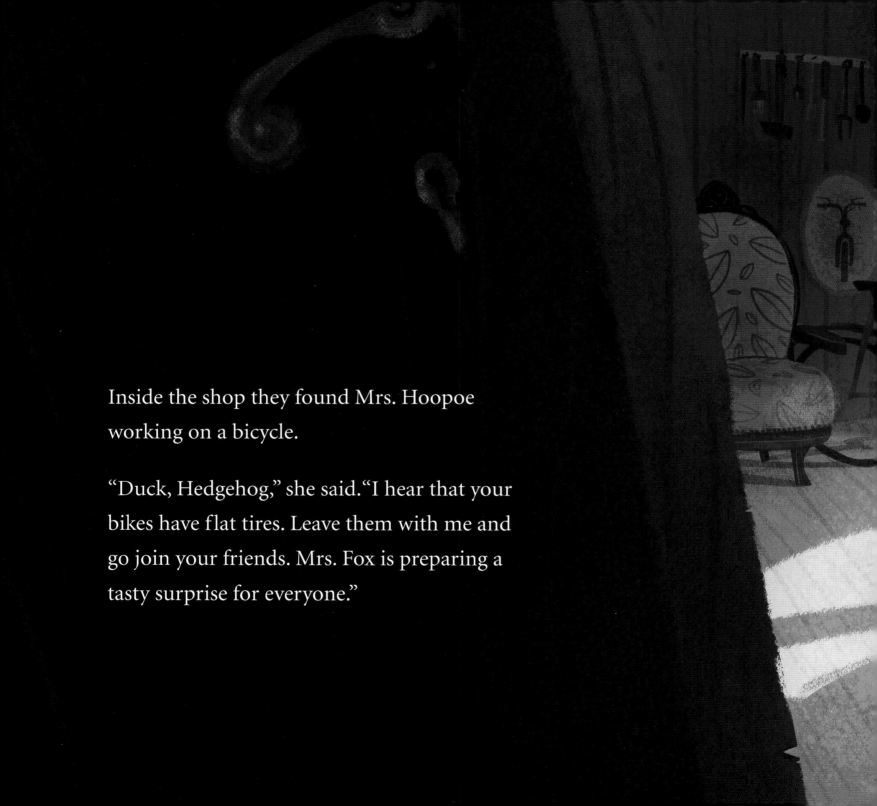

Inside the shop they found Mrs. Hoopoe
working on a bicycle.

"Duck, Hedgehog," she said. "I hear that your
bikes have flat tires. Leave them with me and
go join your friends. Mrs. Fox is preparing a
tasty surprise for everyone."

Duck and Hedgehog joined the others.

A short time later, out came Mrs. Hoopoe and Mrs. Fox carrying a tray of glasses filled with sparkling raspberry juice.

"Hi, Duck! Hi, Hedgehog!" said Mrs. Fox, as she served juice to everyone. "I walked past the raspberry bush on the hill and saw that the fruit was very ripe. I knew that it was about to spoil, so I picked it and made juice for everyone. Please drink up and enjoy!"

"I don't believe it!" said Duck in astonishment. Hedgehog clinked his glass of raspberry juice against Duck's glass, winked, and announced: "Let's drink to good friends!"

Everyone raised their glasses and toasted: "To good friends!"

And the raspberry juice was tasty.

And the shade was pleasant.

And the company was good.

And everyone was very happy.

Also available from Green Bean Books

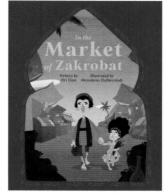

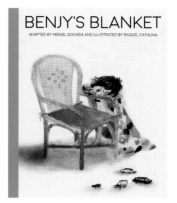

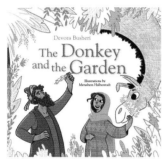

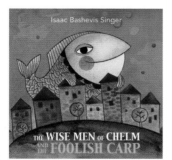

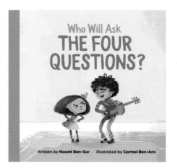

Also available from Green Bean Books

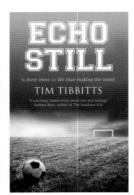

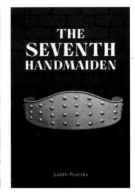

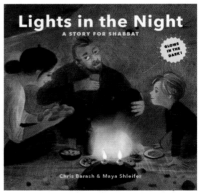

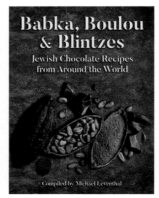